MUFFIN TOP

CAPRICORN COVE SERIES

EVIE MITCHELL

THUNDER THIGHS PUBLISHING

ACKNOWLEDGEMENT OF COUNTRY

I acknowledge the Traditional Custodians of the lands on which I write, the Ngunnawal people, and pay my respect to elders both past and present.

I acknowledge the continued and deep spiritual relationship of the Australian Aboriginal and Torres Strait Islander peoples' to this land, and their unique cultural and spiritual relationships to the land, waters and seas and their rich contribution to society.

Always was, always will be.

To my husband,
Every time I dedicate a book to you, a muffin gets
eaten.
By me.
I'm the one eating all the muffins.
#NoRegrets

MUFFIN TOP

Honey

For years my mumma's been at me to lose some extra pounds. To shape up, slim down, and look like the pageant queen she'd always wished me to be. But everyone knows the best part of the muffin is the top—and baby, I'm delicious as I am.

I hadn't planned on running into my high school crush at a Halloween party while dressed as a cupcake. One glance, and I was ready for my high school crush to take a bite.

Pity Sheriff Tristan Rodriguez avoided baked goods like the plague.

Tristan

Returning to the small town I'd left behind hadn't exactly been in my life plan. Also not in the plan? Becoming the town's most eligible bachelor. I now had more offers for baked goods and home-cooked dinners than I'd ever need.

I hadn't been tempted to taste even one until I ran into my high school crush, Honey

Jameson. The curvy siren looked good enough to eat.

Now she's on my mind, and all I can think about is how to get one little lick. But the thing is, after one taste? I want to devour her whole.

Warning: This marshmallow-y piece of cotton candy sexiness involves a good boy ready to go bad, a curvy woman loving her body, and the fulfilling of some high school wet dreams. Get thee a good guy (or a bad one), maybe a rich chocolate muffin or three, and settle in—this second-chance story will literally burn your sheets.

1

Honey

Even I had to admit I looked delicious. I floated around the bar, hips swaying in time to the band, enjoying the festivities.

Halloween was one of my favourite days of the year. But then, I had a bunch of favourites; Christmas, New Year, Valentine's Day, birthdays —any major event, really. If there was an excuse to celebrate, I celebrated.

"Oh, Honey."

I cringed, freezing at the sound of my mother's voice. Mentally girding my loins, I pasted a smile on my face as I turned around. There she was, my stick-thin mother, standing arm-in-arm with my handsome father. They were dressed as

Cinderella and the Prince—post-rescue, of course. Her tiara matched her glittering dress, both of which were paired perfectly with Father's outfit.

"Ah, my distinguished parents. Welcome!" I moved to kiss them, but my mother grabbed my arms, her fingers digging in to my flesh as she held me at arm's length.

"Why didn't you wear the outfit I sent you?" Her sharp rebuke cut through the revelry around us. Heads turned as people glanced our way.

Why am I not wearing the pumpkin outfit you sent me? Hmm, maybe because no one should cover up the deliciousness that is me?

I forced a small laugh, tossing my long hair, sending a cloud of shimmering glitter flying. I went with the easy answer, "it didn't fit."

Her mouth flattened into a thin, pinched line.

"And this," she waved a hand to encompass my outfit. "Does?"

I looked down at my gods damned adorable, not to mention sexy, self.

Pink corset, fluffy multicoloured tutu and knee-high pastel striped socks were paired with white kitten heels. I looked like a delicious cupcake—if a cupcake could turn people on, which, depending on the level of icing, was entirely possible.

"Yes," I replied, feeling my joy start to ebb.

Shake it off, Honey. Don't let her get to you. Shields up!

My mother was what I liked to call an emotional vampire. She received sustenance by sucking the life and happiness out of the rest of us. My father was obviously a soulless zombie to have lived with her for so long.

She sniffed, dropping my arms. "You should really cover up. No one wants to see your cellulite."

It was kind of sad, but the comment didn't really hurt. Not after years of this kind of treatment.

"Thanks for your advice," I told her, stepping away. "But I'm not wearing this for others. I'm wearing this for—"

"Agatha!" my mother interrupted, waving briskly at someone behind me, attempting to flag her down. "How was your vacation?"

And like a magical being from hell, she disappeared into the crowd, taking another little piece of my joy with her.

My father trailed behind her like a baby duck, not even acknowledging my existence.

No surprise there.

There were three children in my family—the

heir, the spare, and the I-don't-care. In that race, I sat dead last. I always had, always would. I'd accepted my place long ago.

I didn't like it, but I'd accepted it.

The band started playing a cover of Taylor Swift's *Shake It Off*, my mood once again lifting.

"Okay, music gods. I hear you." I shimmied my way back onto the dance floor, determined to ignore the couples around me making out.

My friends shifted, making way for me to rejoin their circle.

There were five of us—if you didn't count my besties' men, who were all hanging out at the bar watching us with amused expressions while they nursed a beer.

"You okay?" Ella asked, yelling to be heard over the music.

Ella reminded me of a Venus come to life with her long mahogany locks, overly abundant curves, and sensual, knowing smile. Tonight she was dressed as a pirate complete with a bustier that did amazing things for her breasts. I'd already seen her fiancé eyeing off her abundance of creamy skin like she was his last meal.

I nodded at my friend. "Not gonna let her pull me into her drama."

"She's such a bitch," Blue yelled, shaking her head. "You need to cut her off."

Bluebelle had been named for her white

grand aunt, a woman whose name might put you in mind of a pale milking maid frolicking through the hills while singing show tunes. But the moment you met Blue, you realised how wrong your perception was.

Her yards of thick curls had been painstakingly tamed into a long smooth waterfall of hair that she'd sprayed a reddish colour. With her body encased in a Jessica Rabbit blood-red shimmer dress, her curves were on display as her two men—Drake and Dane—who watched her appreciatively from the bar.

"It's fine." I flicked a hand dismissively. "I'm done with her."

"Good," yelled Anika as she slung an arm around my shoulders and swayed slightly into me. "Tonight is for fun! It's the first Halloween Ella, and I have had off since we opened this place. Let's party!"

Hilariously dry and irreverent, Anika had zero filters, and I adored her for it. Tonight her long black hair had been interwoven with gold, while gold dust had been brushed over every inch of her visible skin.

She'd explained that she'd decided to come as Anck-su-namun from The Mummy while her fiancé Mac was dressed as Brendan Fraser's character. Apparently, she wanted him to lean into messing up her gold paint later that night.

Each to their own fantasy.

An arm wrapped gently around my waist, and I turned to find Collins watching me with a calm, considering gaze.

The last of our group, Collins, had always been more reserved than the rest of us. She worked as a yoga instructor and physical therapist in my clinic, helping me to transform the lives of our clients.

I adored her, grateful beyond measure that she'd chosen to stay in town when she could be doing bigger and better things.

"You sure?" She asked quietly as the song ended and the band began to transition to the next number.

"I'm good. Promise."

Dressed as the first female Doctor Who, Collins studied me with an expression that wouldn't have looked out of place on the show, her green gaze serious.

"Alright," she said finally, letting me go. "Let's dance."

I threw myself into the music, concentrating on my body. I loved how I moved and relished the way the sound flowed through me. I gave in to the sensation to shuffle, move, sway, dip and jive.

Music had always been a large part of my life, and nights like this reminded me of how free I felt when I was free to connect with sound through movement.

One song flowed into another, then another, and before I knew it, the band was wrapping up for the night, the bar calling for last drinks.

"Damn." I wiped sweat from my brow, beaming at Collins. "That was a killer evening."

"We didn't get men, but we definitely won the dance competition for tonight."

"Amen, sister." Laughing, I slapped palms with her.

Linking arms, Collins and I followed our friends as their partners ushered them out and into the carpark.

"I'm gonna let you fuck me so hard you'll be tasting gold for *weeks*," Anika told Mac, her voice overly loud in the quiet night.

Sniggering, I exchanged a waggle of eyebrows with Collins.

"Let's get you home, Ani," Mac told her, pressing a kiss to her head. "We'll see if you last the ride home before making any plans."

His sweet care in the face of her drunkenness hit me right in that deepest empty hallow, setting off an ache I hoped to find someone to fill.

I wanted what my friends had. Amazing partners who adored them. Who lifted them up. Who made them better, not different.

One day I'll find a man worthy of my level of awesome.

My skin prickled in the cool autumn air as I dug my car key out of the pocket I'd sewn into the underside of the tutu.

"You need a lift?" I asked Collins.

"Nah, the Double Ds promised me a lift home." She tilted her head towards the throuple currently making out across the car park. "If they can pull themselves away."

I chuckled, opening the door of my car. "See you at work on Monday."

"Failing aliens, I'll be there."

I'd originally planned this as a big night out with my girlfriends. We'd agreed to start the night at the Bronze Horseman and try to find a hook up for Collins and I. We'd then retreat to the beach for a bonfire, all of us dancing under the full moon.

Instead, here I was driving my sorry and sober ass home.

Alone.

Again.

I sighed heavily.

At least music never lets me down.

I hit play on my mix, cranking the sound right up, needing to feel the bass thump the loneliness away.

A few miles from home, I rolled to a stop at

an intersection, waiting for an oncoming truck to pass. Shimmying along to Lizzo I was wholey unprepared for a car to hit me from behind.

Thrown forward, my stomach crushed into the steering wheel as my car spun into the intersection—the lights of the oncoming truck a blinding, terrifying white.

Is this how I die? Squashed under a truck while dressed as a delicious baked good?

Winded, crushed and unable to draw breath, I scrunched my eyes shut and braced for impact.

What a way to go. I hope Ani writes my eulogy.

My car jerked again as the truck grazed my bumper, somehow managing to avoid a full collision. Jerked this way and that, my car spun around and around like a ride at a theme park until finally, it jerked to a stop.

Heaving in a breath, I stared out from the middle of the intersection, my hands death gripping the steering wheel as my heart pounded out of my chest.

"Am... am I alive?"

Distantly I heard screaming, slamming doors, and screeching tires.

In a daze, I sat sucking in deep gulping breaths until a woman smacked her hand frantically against the glass of my driver's window, startling me half to death.

"Hey! Hey you!" She screamed, slapping her palm against the glass. "Open up!"

"Jesus!" I choked out, a hand pressing against my poor, pounding chest. "What the fuck?"

I rolled my window down, grimacing as the muscles in my back protested.

"Can I help you?" I asked, dimly registering that I was likely skipping my way toward shock.

"Oh, my gawd," she breathed, her eyes bugging out. "You nearly died. And they just.... They took off!"

"Cops are on their way!" A man yelled at me from the passenger door. He yanked my door open and climbed in to my passenger seat. "Don't worry, we'll get you out."

I blinked, looking down at my body. I wasn't pinned. My car didn't even seem damaged—though I hadn't seen the outside yet.

"I'm okay," I told them. "Everything is fine. I'm not even sore."

At least, not much.

Flashing lights alerted me to the arrival of our local police.

"Over here! She's in shock!" the woman hollered as the officers climbed out.

I sighed, unsnapping my seat belt.

First my parents, now this? Bad things come in

threes. So, what's next? A house fire? An STI? A stalker?

Wait. How hot is the stalker?

I staggered getting out of my car, not because I was hurt, but because the overly helpful stranger decided I needed her to death grip my arm and haul me against her.

"Look!" she squealed, waving frantically at the cops. "The officers are here to help you."

I tugged at my arm, trying to free myself from her tentacles.

"Miss, are you oka—wait. *Honey?*"

My spine went ramrod straight, my head twisting toward the familiar voice.

Hot damn. That is a mountain of a man.

Tall and broad, the officer filled out his uniform in a way I couldn't help but like. He had acres of tanned skin and dark, messy hair. His hands were big, his thick thighs deliciously climbable and bulky. But it was his face that captured my attention—his very gorgeous, very familiar face.

"Tristan?" his name fell from my lips, tasting of bittersweet memories and unrequited love.

"Honey, shit." He reached my side and easily disentangled me from the octo-samaritan to lead me away a few paces. His partner assessed the situation, moving to distract the overly-excited woman with a line of questions.

He held my hand, assessing me with his warm, dark eyes.

"Are you okay?"

I blinked, unable to find the words to express just how okay I was now that he held my hand.

Tristan had grown since our last encounter at our high school graduation. We'd been wearing robes that had flattered no one and smiles a mile wide. I'd been valedictorian, he'd been class president. We'd been friends. Study buddies. Mutual acquaintances who circled each other but never quite matched up. I'd wanted to confess my love to him before he left for college. Instead, I'd signed his yearbook with a suitably generic 'stay in touch,' followed by my cell number.

He'd never called.

Despite the time between now and then, he hadn't changed that much. Sure, he stood taller and broader, with a five o'clock shadow that didn't quit and a look in his eyes that hadn't been there all those years ago. But overall, he was still the same devilishly handsome man I'd known back then.

Maybe.

"Honey? You okay? What hurts?"

I snapped out of my daze. "Oh, yeah. I'm fine. Great. Peachy." I beamed at him, immensely conscious of the hella-sexy outfit I wore.

Take that, Mother.

His badge glinted in the dim light, drawing my eyes to it.

"You're the new sheriff?"

He looked down at the metal badge pinned to his chest. "Yeah, officially started last month."

"Oh." I hadn't realized. Why hadn't I realized?

You've had other things on your mind.

"Congratulations." I blinked up at him, trying to shake this strange fog away. "And welcome back, I guess."

His lips twitched as if he were fighting a smile. "What are you meant to be? Your costume?"

"A sexy cupcake."

He arched an eyebrow but didn't comment. Instead, he reached into his back pocket and pulled out a notepad. He flicked it open, writing the date and my name. He paused, glancing down at me.

"Are you still a Jameson?"

I chuckled, my cheeks flushing. "If that's your way of asking if I'm single, Sheriff, then the answer is yes. Still single and ready to mingle."

He smiled, and I checked out his ring finger while he finished writing my name.

Not married—wait. Are cops allowed to wear rings while on duty? Mental note: google that later.

"You been drinking tonight?"

"No, sir." I grimaced as the muscles in my shoulders and neck began to protest.

Great, whiplash, just what I need.

"Where's home?" he asked, watching me begin to stretch.

"Wherever you are." I froze mid-twist, my gaze glued to his face.

Did I really just say....?!?

Tristan blinked twice fumbling with the notepad in his hands and nearly dropping it.

Oh gods. Oh no. Oh gods. Did I...? I did. I... Oh no. Ohhh no. Nonon-nonononononononononononononono no!

This was a nightmare. Could the world just open up and swallow me whole? Which god did I need to petition to have that happen right now?

See? Bad things always happen in threes.

2

Tristan

I didn't know how to react to Honey's declaration. On one hand, there was the good guy in me who thought I should save her the embarrassment and blow it off, dismiss her comment as nothing but shock and maybe a little head trauma.

But the bad inner voice I tried to suppress whispered darker thoughts.

Honey's thick blonde hair, startling blue eyes, and delicious abundance of curves looked just as good now as the day I'd left town. Better, if I was completely honest. The woman looked like sex in heels. I didn't have any clue what the hell a sexy cupcake was meant to look like, but this woman looked good enough to eat.

Ask her for a taste....

"Boss?"

My deputy saved me from my dark thoughts.

"Just got a notification, the car that hit Honey is heading along the coast road. Looks like a drunk driver. He's smashed into three cars already and—"

I held up my hand, cutting him off. In the distance, I could hear the ambulance sirens coming toward us.

"You okay?" I asked Honey, as, for the first time, the chaffing weight of responsibility settled on my shoulders. I'd never felt this way about my job before. Not once.

"Fine. I'll pop in tomorrow and give you my statement." She sent me a winning smile. "Go get your man, Sheriff."

I noticed her shiver in the cool night air, her arms crossing over her bountiful chest, hands rubbing briskly.

"Here." I shrugged out of my jacket, handing it to her. "You can return it when you come in."

"Thanks."

"Boss!"

I shot her a wink and then jogged to the waiting car just as the ambulance arrived. Caleb flicked on the lights as the paramedics jumped out, heading toward Honey.

I looked at her, finding her gaze on me. Honey smiled, raising a hand as Caleb pulled us away, continuing to wave farewell as I watched in the rearview mirror.

"She's a nice girl. That car'll have to be towed, though," Caleb muttered as he navigated the streets, speeding through our small town.

"Mmm," I murmured, listening to the updates coming from dispatch.

"Shame about her family," Caleb said, jerking the wheel to make a hard left.

I clutched the 'oh shit' handle, gritting my teeth as I slid against the door.

"Her family?"

"Yeah, her mumma is like a fucking praying mantis. Feasts off the bodies of the boys Honey brings home. I've heard the rumours. Ain't no one made it past one dinner with that family."

"Huh," I muttered, raising an eyebrow. "So, she doesn't date?"

"Not since high school," Caleb informed me cheerfully. "Damn shame, too. That woman is certifiably sexy."

I glanced at him, surprised at his comment. I'd always thought of Honey as larger than life and twice as fine. But many men would take one look at her curves—not exactly in fashion at the moment—and turn away.

Their loss.

"What?" Caleb asked, catching my glance. "The woman is hilarious, charismatic, and knows how to work her body. Not to mention gives a damn good at massage." He rolled his shoulder, the car still barreling down the road. "Pulled a muscle trying to catch a drunk tourist last year. She fixed me right up."

"She's a masseuse?"

"Nah, physical therapist. Got her own clinic and everything down on East Street. Does remedial massage and that thing where you sit cross-legged and hum."

"Yoga? Meditation?"

"Both," he agreed. "My girlfriend goes once a week. Wants me to come, but I'm not about to become town gossip by getting a boner in public from watching my girl dance around in spandex for an hour."

I snickered, imagining Caleb attempting a downward dog.

Not pretty.

"Heads up." Caleb nodded at the road ahead. "Looks like we found our guy."

We fell in behind the perp, lights and siren blaring as the drunk driver's car swerved slowly from one side of the road to the other.

"Is he... slowing down?" Caleb asked.

I could walk faster than this chase.

"Looks like it." I unclipped my seat belt. "Stop here, gonna see if I can pull him out."

The next ten minutes were surprisingly uneventful. I jogged alongside the car and managed to pull the drunk driver from the slowest-moving car chase in history.

Noting the numerous empty beer bottles rolling around in the footwell, it didn't surprise me that he smelled like a distillery.

Handcuffed and so drunk he'd passed out, we carried him to the patrol car, pouring the idiot into the back before heading back to the station.

"So," Caleb said as we finished writing up our report. "You gonna wait for Ms. Jameson to come here, or you gonna pursue her?"

I raised an eyebrow. "You matchmaking deputy?"

He grinned. "Unashamedly so."

I laughed. "Guess I better go find me some Honey then."

◆ ◆ ◆

The morning shift after Halloween always had an interesting cluster of people in holding, and today was no different. Four frat boys dressed as Hugh Heffner's slept off last night's drinking effort. Two women—one dressed as a rabbit, the other a playboy bunny—were separated. They'd been arrested wrestling in the flower bed of one of the local matrons. Something about a miscommunication with costumes that escalated to physicality. Joining them were a Joker, Spiderman, three Nuns, and a guy wearing a lot of stuffed cat heads.

Yep. Apparently, he was a 'pussy magnet.'

Nice try, pal.

I checked over the paperwork, noting that the drunk driver who'd hit Honey was still locked up.

I walked to the front desk. "Jason, has Mr. Morrison contacted someone to come bail his ass out?"

Jason checked the system. "He's called the place he was staying. His wife is in America visiting family. He's here on some work thing. Said his wife is the reason he drinks."

"Where's he staying?"

"Up at the Adventure place. They said they'll contact the wife, then give us an update."

"Adventure place?" I asked, making a note about the guy being from one of the southern islands. I glanced at my watch. The courthouse would open in an hour; he'd be arraigned later today.

"I forget you ain't been here forever. So, Drake Andrews and Dane Butler—you might've gone to school with them? Anyway, they left the Marines and moved back here. Turns out they're shacked up with Bluebell McKenney—you remember her, right? She's a nurse at the clinic in town. They do diving, hiking, high ropes, and corporate wilderness bonding and shit. They're all together, too, like in the biblical sense. But the town is cool with it. Not sure how it all works, to be honest, but—"

I sighed, wishing I'd never asked. Jason may be a great receptionist, working our front desk and keeping most of the nonsense reports from the local geriatric neighbourhood watch off my desk, but the kid could talk underwater.

"Oh, speaking of. That's them." Jason nodded at the front door.

I turned, watching two large men walking toward us. They'd been a few years ahead of me in school, and both of them had only moved to the Cove in their teens. If memory served, they'd been foster kids, living with the McKenney's for a few years before heading off to the Marines. But that was as much as I knew about them—barring the info dump Jason just unloaded on me.

Oh, and that they enjoyed skinny-dipping with Bluebell McKenney. That was certainly one story Jason didn't know.

They made it to the desk, giving me a polite nod, then turned to Jason.

"Heard you got one of our guests here?"

"Surely do, Dane," Jason said brightly. He turned to me. "The Sheriff here picked your boy up last night."

I leaned against the desk. "DUI. He's drying out in lock-up."

Drake sighed, shaking his head.

"His wife is visiting family in Florida. She's authorized us to make decisions until she can get here." His mouth twisted. "Though I'm not sure the guy's gonna be eager for her to get here. The woman was mighty angry that she's gotta cut this trip short for his shit."

I chuckled.

"How's this play out, Sheriff?" Dane asked.

"Well, unless someone posts bail, he'll be kept here until the arraignment later today," I explained. "He hit a car, nearly causing a major accident. He caused damage to a few parked vehicles and blew over the legal limit. Well over. This looks like his first offence, but the judge may decide he's a flight risk. Has his wife arranged a lawyer?"

"She asked us to call her once we got here. She's on the phone trying to track someone down."

I nodded. "Then I'll leave you all to it."

The entry door beeped just as I moved to step away.

"Sheriff Tristan, perfect timing."

I froze, my body immediately tensing at that voice. I turned, pasting a blank smile on my face.

"Miss Sharp, how can I help you today?"

Hannah Sharp had the kind of predatory gleam in her eye that made me immediately ill at ease. The woman was a piranha dressed in Chanel.

"Sheriff, you know you can call me Hannah. And I bought you some cookies."

She handed me the fabric-wrapped plate. I took it, immediately handing it off to Jason. Jason's eyes twinkled, and he gave me that smirking, knowing grin. I made a face, then turned back.

"Thank you, Miss Sharp. I'm sure my colleagues will enjoy them."

"Yes.... Well, I'll just pop in tomorrow to pick up the plate. What time would be—"

"Oh, no need," Jason interjected. "Just give me one minute, and I'll have it back."

Before Hannah could protest, he took off, heading toward the break room.

I shoved my hands in my pockets, waiting

awkwardly while Hannah attempted to make small talk. I noticed her complete avoidance of Drake and Dane, who both frowned at her.

"Here you go," Jason gallantly handed the plate back. "Better get in there quick, Sheriff. They're going fast."

"Perhaps—" Hannah started, but someone called my name from the bullpen.

"Sorry, duty calls. Thanks for the cookies," I told her, nodding to both her and the two men.

I pivoted, beating a quick retreat. I headed immediately to Caleb, finding him stuffing his mouth.

"Yo, Sheriff," he said around a mouth full of cookies. "This is your third delivery today."

Don't I know it.

I'd been back in town for three months. Most of that, I'd spent working out accommodation and trying to support my mother, who was still grieving dad's loss. Then I'd run in the Sheriff election, and now I was ta month into the job, and the baked goods didn't stop coming.

None of this was in the plan.

I ran a hand through my hair, not exactly displeased with my life, but certainly unsettled.

"Your girl called. She can't make it today. Said she'll try to stop by tonight."

I hesitated. "I'm going to take myself off this case. You good to lead?"

Caleb's eyebrows raised in surprise. "Any particular reason?"

Because the woman looked good enough to eat last night? Because her outfit made me want to decorate her breasts with icing and lick it off? Because I jerked myself off three times to thoughts of her?

"I know Honey personally," I answered casually. "Don't want that to be used against us."

"Uh-huh." Caleb leaned back in his chair, a smirk on his lips. "You know she got a ride into work with Paulette today? They're neighbours."

Paulette was one of our best detectives. I filed that piece of info away for later.

Caleb glanced at his watch. "It's nearly midday, Sheriff. And I know it was a late night for both of us, but you're the idiot who chose to work the morning shift. How about you head off early? We got this."

I glanced around, mentally tallying the work I still needed to do against my desire to see Honey.

"I might do that. I've got a few loose ends to tie up first." I clasped Caleb on the shoulder. "Thanks."

"No problem." He winked at me. "And Honey works up on East Street, just in case you've forgotten."

"Jesus, Caleb. At least try to be subtle about it. This isn't an episode of the Bachelor."

"Dude, I would be the best matchmaker in history."

I rolled my eyes, chuckling. "Yeah, right."

3

Tristan

Any warmth the afternoon sunlight may have been trying to produce was hidden by clouds that muddied the sky. The smell of rain hung heavy in the air, though we'd yet to receive a drop.

I looked up at the storefront of Honey's clinic. I'd taken Caleb's offer, leaving early to nap and shower and now found myself wandering East street, counting down the minutes until her clinic closed. I knew she was still there; Caleb had fed me the intel. His girlfriend was a surprisingly perfect source for Honey-related matters.

Capricorn Cove Physical Therapy and Sports Clinic was scrawled in thick black professional-looking letters across the glass frontage. The building itself was painted blue and white, fitting in nicely with the fancy heritage boutiques on either side. Like most of the other storefronts in town, it held a themed window display.

I laughed, taking in the skeleton with one leg propped on a jack-o-lantern stretching, a ghost sitting on a fitness ball, and a werewolf in child's pose on a yoga mat.

Some things had changed since coming home. It seemed Honey wasn't one of them.

Every season without fail, her locker had been an explosion of colour and comedy. She'd been on every school decorating committee and took every excuse to celebrate holidays and seasons—hell, even her lunch boxes had been themed. Back in school, I'd noticed things like that. Her lunchboxes and how she often wore clothing and jewellery that reflected her moods. I'd enjoyed covertly observing her, enjoyed watching her smile and laugh, and occasionally feeling that warmth directed my way.

A memory snuck up on me, an image of Honey dutifully hanging love hearts all over her locker. Valentine's Day, senior year. I'd finally plucked up the courage to ask her out. The card had sat heavy in my hand, my sweaty palms pressed into the pockets of my jeans as I tried to casually stroll toward her. Her eyes lit up, and she gave me a smile, her hand lifting to offer a little wave when she saw me.

My heart had pounded loudly in my ears, my tongue dry and far too large for my mouth. I'd swallowed, unable to get the words out. I'd wanted to pause, lean against the locker beside her, and then ask her out. Instead, I'd offered her what I think was more of a grimace than a smile and strode straight past. I'd never tried again.

You were a fucking chicken.

I couldn't deny the accusation. Sure, I'd been class president, captain of the football team, and voted the nicest guy in our graduating year. But I'd also been exactly that—a nice guy. And nice guys, I'd learned, finished last.

It hadn't helped that I'd had a monobrow, buck teeth, and acne. Sure, I'd been popular, but I'd never felt attractive enough to ask out the women I'd crushed on the most. And I'd crushed hard on Honey Jameson.

Still do, it seems.

A little over a decade later, my looks were no longer questionable. A few years of braces and a regular wax of the old eyebrows had left me feeling better about my appearance than that self-conscious kid I'd left behind.

The curtain backdrop for the picture window moved. It bobbled for a second, then slowly lifted, revealing Honey, inch by beautiful inch. Her bottom half was encased in skintight Halloween-themed sports leggings—cheerful dancing skeletons covering her thick legs. Her top was a black professional polo shirt with the clinic's logo embroidered on the breast. She'd pulled her blond hair back into a messy high ponytail, a few strands slipping free to fall gently around her face.

She blinked, catching me standing there watching her. A grin spread across her face, lighting her eyes. She made a *come here* hand gesture, nodding toward the door, then winced slightly, her hand immediately reaching to rub the nape of her neck.

Frowning at her discomfort, I made my way around.

Whiplash? If so, why is she at work?

She met me at the door, a welcoming grin firmly in place.

"Sheriff, come on in." She swept a hand out to encompass the waiting room. "Welcome to my humble empire."

The outside mimicked the exterior of the building, with white and blue weatherboard mixed with brick and glass. I'd expected the inside to have the same traditional beach cottage feel. Instead, it felt like stepping into an exclusive day spa. Soft lighting, wood floors, and bronze highlights mixed with lush greenery and calming seascape graphics. A diffuser sat on the reception desk, quietly misting a citrus and lemongrass scent into the air while relaxing rainforest sounds played softly in the background.

"Wow." I paused in the centre of the room, taking in the impressive set-up. "This is incredible."

Honey flushed, looking pleased. "It's taken me a while to get here, but it's nearly exactly as I want it. We're a whole of body service—we do physical therapy, help people bounce back from injuries or recover from poor health, and we also do relaxation. I find that patients respond better when they're calm and in the right mindset."

She rolled her shoulders, wincing a little.

"You okay?"

She sighed, offering a rueful smile. "Tight. I'd normally ask one of my therapists to loosen me up, but Collins is off sick, and Rowan is on vacation. Between Shandra and me, we've had a full workload today." She turned to the hall. "Come on, I'll show you around."

Honey led me through her clinic, pointing out the three treatment rooms, one exam room, and the small office with a kitchenette and toilet off the side. At the back of the hall were two large rooms separated by a thick soundproof wall.

"This is our exercise room."

Large windows let in light, while exercise equipment such as weights, treadmills, and stationary bikes sat in straight lines. She flicked the lights off, leading me into the next room.

With her hand on the door handle, Honey turned, giving me bright eyes and a huge smile.

"This is our newest build. We've only been operating this space for the last three months, but I'm really excited to be offering our clients Pilates and yoga classes. We've also hired a trained mindfulness coach to offer meditation courses. We've offered a few courses now and have been overwhelmed by the response."

Taking a subtle deep breath, she opened the door, flicking on a light switch. Soft lighting gently warmed the room. The space was mostly empty, but for the wood floors, warm colours, and tall windows covered by the same roller blinds as those hanging at the clinic's front.

"Has a good feel," I commented, walking in and catching the scent of sandalwood and lavender in the air. This place felt calming, and I immediately knew this meant a lot to her.

"Why did you expand?"

She walked over to the diffuser that sat on one of the small inbuilt wall platforms, turning it off. As she walked around the room, doing the same with the other two, she spoke softly, revealing her passion for her patients and her work.

"Our client's minds are just as important as their bodies. The mind is just as essential for healing the body as any exercise I encourage my patients to do. If you come to my clinic stressed, tight or worried, no massage or stretch or exercise will relieve you. You'll just walk right back out and become worse. So, we decided to expand and offer these classes. Try and give people the mental tools at the same time we give them the physical."

She waved a hand around, encompassing the room.

"I built this addition because I wanted everything to be completely accessible for every client who walks, rolls, or shuffles through our door. We could have gone up and changed the top floor attic into a studio, but it wouldn't have been accessible to everyone. So, we bumped out. More money and more time, but the end result is inclusive, which is what my clients deserve. Everyone should have access to peace, and this room, the programs we offer here, will hopefully give them a little slice of that feeling."

"I get that."

I followed her from the room, heading back

to the reception area. Back at the entry, I hovered awkwardly, shoving my hands in my jean pockets, glancing around, desperate to stay longer. My gaze narrowed in on the box of decorations spilling across the floor.

"Are you redoing the display?"

"Oh!" She practically skipped to the box to pull a fall wreath free. "Yeah, Halloween's over, so I'm going with a fall theme for November. I've settled on Star Wars." She reached back into the box and pulled an old cloak free. "See? It's the ghost of Obi-Wan!"

"Is Star Wars a fall theme?"

She tilted her head, considering my question. "Maybe not directly, but the colours and mystique work for this time of year. I always think fall is a little dark but a little magic. You know?"

I grinned, squatting down to dig through the box. "I like that you're still into seasonal decorations. It was always one of my favourite things about you."

She froze. "You remember that?"

"Honey, I remember everything."

Our gazes met and held. There were a million thoughts and emotions flickering behind that look—and I wanted to decipher them all.

"Tristan," Honey asked softly. "Are you here to get my statement or your jacket back?"

"Both," I admitted. "But that can wait till tomorrow. How about I give you a hand tonight with the display?"

She bit her lip, and for a second, I thought she was going to refuse.

"I'd actually really like that."

Honey's quiet admission left me feeling like I'd won the damn Super Bowl.

I lugged boxes, helping her pack away the Halloween items and hang the new decorations. I listened as she described how the town had changed in the years I'd been gone.

"You know, I'm surprised I didn't hear you were back," she paused, hands extended above her head, balancing a garland of leaves. "I mean, I've been busy with the build, but I didn't think I was that busy to have missed the incredible Tristan's return."

She sent me a saucy wink before turning back to drape the garland.

"Incredible, hmm?" I shifted, holding the ladder steady for her. This position gave me an uninterrupted view of her ass—perfection.

"Oh, don't pretend like you don't know you are. The many accolades at school, getting into college with a full ride, becoming a detective in record time." She chuckled. "You've become quite the hometown hero."

"I doubt that."

She finished pinning, and I let go, moving to give her space to climb down. Once safely back on the floor, she crossed her arms over her chest, giving me a large grin.

"Your mum came in a few times. You and your brother were all she'd talk about." She shrugged, grimacing at the movement. "It's nice that your mum is so proud of you."

"I don't know." I tugged a small leaf free from her hair. "I think it's in the rule book for parents to be abnormally proud of their kids."

"I can tell you categorically that's not true." She turned, reaching for the next set of decorations.

I remembered Caleb's comment from last night about her parents disapproving of her boyfriends.

"Why would your parents not be proud of you? Look at all you've achieved." I wave a hand around, gesturing at the room. "Babe, this is impressive. By all accounts, you're a successful businesswoman, kick-ass therapist, and a genuinely caring human being."

She blinked at me for a moment, then flushed, looking away. "That's really nice of you to say."

I crouched beside her, waiting till she looked at me.

"It's not nice. It's the truth. You've always

been intelligent, funny, and charismatic. People want to be around you because you're like—" I tried to think of an analogy that didn't sound corny. "A firefly."

She snorted, a surprised laugh bursting free. "What?"

"You know." I made a floating motion with my hand. "They're reminders of summer. Of long days and great memories. They're magical. They sparkle. They bring people joy. You want to catch them and hold that magic in your hand, but you know if you do, you'll break it." I shrugged. "You're like that. Magical. A little mysterious. Everyone wants to be around you."

She looked stunned, her eyes wide, her mouth slack. She swallowed, then swallowed again.

"That's... that is honestly the nicest thing anyone has ever said to me." She looked away, taking a deep breath before turning back to me, a small smile I'd never seen before on her lips. "Just for the record, I don't break easily."

I grinned, and for a long moment, all we did was stand in the display window, smiling at each other. Surprisingly, even that devil voice inside me felt okay with this moment.

"So." She finally broke eye contact, reaching for some clear fishing line. "What brought you back? Last I heard, you were living it large down on the south island. Cape Hardgrave, right?"

"Yeah." I blew out a breath, returning to the giant skeleton I'd been tasked with wrangling into a wizard robe. "It's a shit story."

"I've got nowhere to be."

I frowned, keeping my hands busy as I bent a skeleton's elbow, shoving its arm into the sleeve of a cloak.

"The short, sad story is Dad died, and Mum just doesn't know how to cope without him. She fell into a depression, rang me hysterical one night because she didn't know how to pay the electricity bill, and the company had turned the power off." I shook my head. "I moved back home and started working for the local station about three months ago. The old Sheriff had decided it was time to retire but didn't have anyone with enough experience to take over. I figured I'd already moved back; may as well throw my hat in the ring." I shot her a wry grin. "Never expected to be offered the damn thing."

"Was the recruitment round close?"

I chuckled. "No. I was the only applicant."

She laughed, then sobered. "I'm sorry about your dad. I attended his funeral. He was a good man."

That hole in my chest began to ache. "Yeah, he was."

We decorated silently for a while, murmuring softly when we needed something, and positioning the display just so.

"I think we're done," Honey said, stepping back and putting her hands on her hips.

We both looked at the display with a critical eye. Fall colours, leaves, and pumpkins framed the skeleton in its Jedi robe. Standing in warrior pose, arm outstretched it threw a zap of the force across the window—represented by twinkling fairy lights—to wrap around a scraggly scarecrow who was balancing precariously on a black yoga ball. The scene was both clever and humorous. Strangely, it also made perfect sense for her business.

"I like it," she declared. Honey bumped me with her hip. "Thanks for staying to help."

"No problem."

She moved and then groaned, one hand coming up to massage the back of her neck. "I'm glad you offered. Not sure I could have got it done by myself tonight."

I caught her hand, gently pulling her closer. When only two inches separated us, I reached up, brushing stray hairs from her cheek. Honey's bright blue eyes were wide as she stared at me in—surprise? Confusion? Shock?

The devil in me awakened, whispering temptations that I could no longer deny.

"You offer relaxation to your clients," I whispered. "But you're tight right now."

She blinked at me slowly. "I'll try to get some time with one of my team tomorrow. Hopefully, Collins is back on board."

"How about," I slid a hand up her arm, moving to rest it on the nape of her neck. "You tell me what to do. I can't guarantee it'll be perfect, but it should help a little with the tension."

"I—I don't know—" she stammered. "I mean—"

I gently applied pressure to the back of her neck, easily finding the tight ball of muscles. She groaned, her eyes closing as I continued my ministration.

"Okay," she whispered, eyes still closed. "But only because this feels amazing."

She opened one eye, her lips lifting in a cheeky grin. "But no one can ever know I let an unqualified therapist as hot as you work here. The line would be out the door, but I'd get sued for your lack of technique by next week."

I chuckled, keeping up the pressure. "I'm not interested in helping out the single ladies of this town. Just you."

She laughed, stepping back and moving down the hall to one of the treatment rooms. I followed her like a lost little lamb, unashamedly checking her out in the process.

"Don't lie, Sheriff. I asked around about you today and heard all about your baked goods harem."

I groaned, pausing in the doorway to watch her walk around the room. With quick, efficient movements, she set up the therapy bed with fresh towels and turned a small pot on to warm the massage oil.

"I never asked for the food. And I've never taken anyone up on the dinner offers." Though I liked the fact she'd asked around about me.

"It must be so hard being the most eligible bachelor in town." She threw a wink my way.

Harder than you'd think, babe.

My cock twitched, enjoying her sass a little too much.

"Okay." She studied the set-up for a moment, then nodded, immediately wincing once again. "We're good to go."

"Where do you need me?"

"Give me a second to take my top off and settle on the bed. I'll call when you can turn back around."

I blinked slowly, not quite comprehending what she'd just said. "Excuse me?"

"Oh." Honey bit her pink lip. "I'm sorry. I thought—this is the way we normally—"

"It's fine. Sorry, I just... I didn't realise you'd be okay with getting semi-naked for me."

We both hovered awkwardly for a moment.

"Here, let me turn around." I spun on my heel, crossing my arms and willing my dick to settle the fuck down.

Behind me, I heard Honey move. There was a rustle of clothing, a creak of the bed, and then the sound of her settling.

"Okay, I'm ready."

I turned and was assailed by skin. So much gorgeous, pale, beautiful skin.

This must be heaven.

4

Honey

I closed my eyes and focused on steadying my breathing and calming my racing pulse.

My body rejected my efforts, my stomach a knot of anticipation.

This is fine. Tristan's just being nice. He's not at all interested in you that way.

I heard him moving around the room.

"Do you want some music on?" His whispered question sent tingles racing up and down my spine.

"Sure," I replied, forcing a casualness I didn't feel.

I heard him fiddle with the stereo and a moment later soft piano music filtered through the room.

I breathed again, listening to him shuffle this way and that. I heard him scoop some oil, coating his hands before he moved toward the bed.

This is fine. You're fine. It's just a massage. Nothing more—

OH MY GOD!

His hands came down to rest on the middle of my back. Immediately my body broke out in goosebumps, every part of me hyper-aware that this man, my teenage crush, was touching me.

TRISTAN IS TOUCHING ME!!

Using slow, gentle strokes, he covered my back in the warm oil.

"You'll have to guide me from here," he whispered. "I could just keep doing this, but I'm unsure how effective it'd be." He brushed his hands up my back in semi-circles, emphasising his point.

"Actually, your technique isn't bad." I sunk deeper into the treatment table, beginning to relax. "But try a little more pressure."

"Like this?" His hands slowed, but his thumbs and palms pressed into my muscles, kneading the tight knots.

"Perfect," I whispered, enjoying this far too much. "Now, just do what feels natural to you.

I'll tell you if something hurts or doesn't feel good."

He followed my words, his hands running up and down in slow circular motions.

It felt good. So damn good.

I drifted, my mind conjuring up images of cabanas and long massages from Tristan under the sun. All of which lead to—

I let out a needy little moan, tensing as Tristan's hands paused on my lower back.

"Is that good?" he asked gruffly.

"Yeah," I whispered, aching with need and a little embarrassment. "Really good."

His hands slowly worked up and down my back. "Are your eyes closed, Honey?"

"Yes."

He didn't comment for a long moment, then let out a shaky breath. "Fuck, here goes."

I waited, eyes still closed, all my senses attuned to him.

"In high school, I crushed on you hard."

I jolted in surprise under his hands, which paused for a beat and then continued their ministrations.

"I wanted to ask you out, but you were always so...." His voice trailed off. "Vivacious. Larger than life. You were the spotlight, and I was just some guy in the background."

I let out a huffed laugh in disbelief. "Excuse

me? You were the 'it' guy. Class president. Star of the football team. I loved every class I had with you. You were always witty and intelligent and knew how to make me and everyone else feel included. Tristan, I had a crush on you too."

His hands faltered on my back. "Really?"

"Uh, yeah." I shifted to sit, but his hand pressed the middle of my back, keeping me still.

"Stay. I'm not done with you yet." His words had an edge of steel to them, and I quivered under his touch, deliciously aware of the fact I loved the authority in his voice.

"Okay," I paused, unsure of how far to push this. "*Sheriff.*"

"Fuck," he muttered, shifting above me, his hands once again gliding across my skin. "Okay. The way I see it, we got three options."

"Options?"

His hands glided across my skin. "I finish this massage; we lock up, and both go home—never talk about it again."

I frowned, not liking that at all.

"Option two, we finish this massage; we lock up, but I take you out to dinner this week."

Oh, I liked that.

"And option three?" I asked, my voice un-usually husky.

"You let me turn you over, peel these leg-gings from your body and massage your pussy.

Then we lock up, and I make you breakfast tomorrow."

Option three. I want option three!

My body, already aching with need, tightened to full desperate arousal at his words. God, I wanted this. I wanted him. I wanted all of it.

"Your choice, babe."

"Three," I didn't hesitate. "I want—" I swallowed, my mouth suddenly dry. "I want you to touch me."

"Turn over."

He pulled the towel up, holding it between us like a curtain, blocking his view. I rolled over, settling into place. He draped the towel back over me, hiding my body from his view. If the situation weren't so hot, I'd probably giggle at the thought of Tristan preserving my modesty after his proposition.

"You can say no at any point," he told me, his beautiful dark eyes meeting mine in the dim light.

"I know."

"Good. Close your eyes."

My lids drifted shut, and I forced myself to take long, deep breaths.

Tristan didn't go straight for my legs. Instead, he stood at my head, his hands working the tight muscles at my neck and shoulders.

"Breathe, babe. Relax. Let me take care of

you." His words were delivered in a low tone that felt like a caress to my soul. I loved how he made me feel, both languidly relaxed and tensely aroused. It was a feeling I'd never experienced before—both achingly sweet and deliciously erotic.

Tristan worked his way down my body, from my neck and shoulders down one arm and then the other. As he finished with my final finger, he shifted, his hands dancing lightly across the towel covering me.

"Ready?"

I nodded, my tongue suddenly too thick for my mouth, making speech impossible.

He left the towel in place and moved to my feet.

"Lift up."

I followed his command, my eyes scrunched shut, my breathing now beleaguered as I thrust up, giving him the space to pull my leggings and underwear down.

I heard him suck in a breath as he revealed my skin. I was tempted to peek but kept my eyes closed, lost in this dark erotic fantasy.

"Beautiful," he whispered as he pulled my clothes away. I heard him move, heard the clothing drop to the floor, and then his hands were on my feet. His thumbs pressed into the arch of my foot, and I moaned with pleasure.

"Relax, Honey. I just wanna make you feel good. Remember, you can stop me at any time."

I had to give the man credit. When he'd said massage, I'd expected a quick ten-minute rub. Instead, I was getting a full body, and I couldn't have been happier.

Sure, we were likely breaking about eight hundred health and licensing codes, but I really couldn't find it in me to care. His hands were wonderful, his occasional directive both seductive and gruff. Everything about him spoke to me.

His hands glided slowly up the inside of my thighs, stopping a hairsbreadth away from my core.

I shifted restlessly on the bed; all sense of modesty now gone. The man could have whatever he wanted so long as he touched me.

Please touch me. Please.

His fingers brushed up my thighs, drifting closer and closer.

Please.

A fingertip brushed against my pussy; pleasure spiralling out as he teased my sensitive skin.

"More," I panted, eyes firmly closed, body on edge. "Please, Tristan. More."

He chuckled, low and deep. "Like this?"

He grazed two fingers over the seams of my pussy, teasing but not really touching.

"Or this?" His finger dipped, finding my clit with the barest of touches before it danced away.

"Yes, that!" I thrust my body up, chasing his hand.

He laughed again, the sound deeply erotic. "As you wish."

His fingers, his clever, naughty fingers, big and blunt and a little rough, returned to my clit. They teased, circling, pressing, rubbing in a way that felt oh-so-good.

I begged. I panted. I moaned. I wanted it to end. I wanted him to keep touching me forever.

This is Tristan. Tristan is touching you. Tristan —who looks like sin on a stick but with a good boy attitude—Tristan.

"Baby, you gonna come for me?" He pressed harder, pulling all sorts of noises from me, playing my body like he was a professional musician, and I, his instrument of choice.

He circled once, twice, and then I broke apart. I bowed off the bed, my body clenching as waves of painful-sweet orgasm washed over me. Pleasure suffused my every cell, imprinting Tristan's name, scent, the feel of him onto my soul.

I returned to myself, slowly becoming aware

of him rubbing soothing circles across my thighs.

"Wow," I whispered, my eyes finally fluttering open to look up at him. "That was a hell of a massage."

He chuckled, stepping back to lean against the vanity, a satisfied smirk on his face. "Feeling relaxed?"

A gloriously lethargic feeling had invaded my limbs. Heavy, but light at the same time. I never wanted to move from the bed.

"Oh, yeah."

He smiled, and I was once again struck by his good looks. This man had boyish good charm coupled with devilishly sexy intentions —a dangerous combination.

"Have to say, I'm impressed you did all that and didn't even try to get a peek of the girls." I waved a hand toward my still towel-covered breasts. "You also didn't ask for anything." I looked pointedly at his crotch. The giant bulge prominent against the material of his dark-wash jeans.

"Tonight was about you." His smile changed to a slightly rueful look. "Besides, I never imagined my first time on a massage bed."

I pushed up, frowning. "Your first time? Do you mean our first time together or...?"

He shrugged. "I'm a virgin. No biggie."

No biggie? He's a virgin? A male virgin capable of delivering pleasure like... like... like that?

"But, how did you... I don't understand."

He quirked an eyebrow.

"I—I mean," I pressed the towel to my chest, heat flushing my cheeks. "I just mean, how you touched me was so... sure. So confident. I would have bet money you'd done that before."

His gaze darkened, eyes burning through me. "Just because I'm a virgin doesn't mean I'm pure, Honey. I've got an imagination and desires like anyone else. I may not have physically touched someone, but that doesn't mean I haven't imagined touching you a million times over."

Touching me?

I swung to sit on the edge of the bed, both aroused and unsure. "Can I help with that?"

"No." He huffed out a breath. "We start now we're not stopping until next week. And I suspect you need to use this room for patients."

"Does this mean we're going to breakfast?"

His lips quirked. "Only if you still want to."

Oh, boy, do I ever.

"I do."

"Good."

I dressed and shut down the clinic while he cleaned up. We met back in reception.

"One problem, I don't have a car. You may

not have heard, but a drunk driver totalled it." I winked.

His lips lifted. "Well, now, I guess I can help with that."

"Oh, thank you, Sheriff. This little lady would be mighty pleased to be saved by you." I fell into him dramatically, grinning widely at the flash of desire in his eyes.

"My place or yours?" he asked, his voice low.

"Mine." I shot him a flirty look. "I have toys."

"Toys, hmm?"

"Mmm, lots of fun toys."

He slung an arm over my shoulder, walking me out. He kept it there as I set the alarm and locked the door. He still had his arm wrapped around me as we got to his car, and he opened the door for me. I moved to get in, but he stopped me.

"Wait." His hands came up, framing my face.

"What?" I raised a hand. "Do I have something on my face?"

"No, baby." Tristan leaned in. "I just need to taste you first."

Our first kiss was in the dim parking lot of my clinic under the crescent moon. He tasted of coffee and chocolate and smelled of massage oil, citrus, and man.

He felt like home.

5

Tristan

Touching Honey had been a religious experience. If she were the goddess, I was her loyal subject, willing to worship at her feet for all time.

Did that make me sound like a pussy? Probably. Did I fucking care? Not a gods damned iota. My woman was all curves and charisma wrapped in a beautiful, loving bow. It might seem fast, but I wanted to put a ring on her finger, a baby in her belly, and a hickey on her neck. I wanted to mark her as mine.

How does she feel about tattoos?

I shook off the thought, fighting the darker side of my personality. I'd kept that motherfucker locked down for years. Oh, sure, he won occasionally and I had a feeling Honey wouldn't mind my kind of dark. That she'd taste sweeter after being ordered around.

"I'm the third on the left."

I followed her direction and parked in her driveway, absently scoping the neighbourhood. The newer development sat on the edge of town. Not a bad area, mostly filled with people who commuted to the city daily. Professionals looking for cheap housing who'd spend their weekdays in the city and their weekends partying down at the docks.

I didn't have any issues with the out-of-towners. They were happy enough to spend money in our town, supporting the local economy. It just sucked that their presence was driving up the cost of living. I'd moved back and invested a large chunk of my savings in buying a home. I knew I wasn't leaving now I was back, not with Mum still desperate for assistance and my brother only just off to college.

Ten years separated Wolf and me. I loved my brother, he was a good son, an awesome brother, and a great friend, but, I had to admit, a lousy boyfriend. I'd heard all about the trail of broken hearts he'd left behind.

Shaking off all thoughts of my brother and

his potential love life dramas, we exited the car and walked up to her entry. Honey paused at her door, a little frown marring her brow.

"Look, it's a little intense inside. Just—don't judge." She worried her bottom lip.

"What, you leave your laundry out?" I joked, resting a hand on her lower back.

"Not quite."

She pushed open the door to reveal what I can only describe as a Halloween-themed fantasy house. A larger and more detailed version of Honey's new window display.

Leaves and branches, lights and costumes decorated every wall, surface, and floor. Her hall had tiny pumpkins strung from the ceiling. An electronic owl carrying a message flapped his little wings in the middle of the display.

As she led me through the house, music began to play softly in the background. In her living room, two broomsticks circled the floor.

"Roombas," Honey admitted with a flush. "I may have gone overboard this year. Pinterest is a dangerous site for me."

I wasn't even sure how to describe this level of creativity, still trying to take everything in.

There were hidden ghosts and ghouls, spider webs and fluttering leaves, cauldrons and sweet-smelling candles just waiting to be lit.

"I shouldn't have brought you here." She wrung her hands together, looking suddenly nervous. "I'm sorry. I know it's too much. It's just—"

"You," I interrupted her. I placed a hand on her elbow, gently drawing her into me. "This is you. You're over-the-top, loud, creative, beautiful." I pressed a kiss to her forehead and another to her cheek. "Babe, this is incredible. It doesn't scare me. It's not too much. It's you. It's perfect."

Her eyes shimmered with unshed tears.

"Hey." I brushed at her cheek with my thumb. "Why are you crying?"

She sniffed, shaking her head. "I just... I always thought I'd have to compromise. That no one could lov—I mean, *like* my whirlwind."

"Ah, Honey." I pulled her close, cradling her in my arms, lending her comfort. This beautiful woman deserved nothing but the best. "I like-love your whirlwind. I always have."

She sniffled briefly, then pulled back, offering a teasing, if watery, grin. "Is this a ploy to get me into bed? Cause you were already getting some."

"Yep. You've found me out." I brushed away a stray tear. "You gotta know I'm crazy about you." I waved a hand around the room, the vacuum broomsticks now bumping against each other. "This says you're the kind of woman who will make my life interesting. You'll decorate our house, light up our life," I grinned. "And most likely leave murder scenes around the house when you're pissed at me."

She laughed; the tears now gone. "Don't tempt me."

"You need another massage?"

She shoved playfully at my chest, then pulled me back down for a kiss. "No, but I do need a good cocking."

I choked.

"What? Not interested in popping that cherry?"

Fuck.

"Get in the bedroom before I spank your juicy ass."

She squealed, turning and running down the hall. I stalked after her, hyper-aware of the log in my pants. My cock throbbed with need, aching and heavy. I shed my shirt as I strode down the hall, following her to the bedroom. I was so ready for this.

I barely noticed the fall décor, my focus entirely taken up by the half-naked woman before me. She'd stripped away her shirt and leggings, leaving her in only a bra and panties. The deep maroon of her underwear offset the pale blush of her skin. She spread her arms wide, giving a slow spin.

"Like what you see?"

Her utter confidence in her own skin was a huge fucking turn-on.

"Fuck, yes." I reached for her, no longer leashing my desire. That darkness in me rose, breaking free of my iron-clad control. "Need to taste your pretty lips."

My mouth descended and met hers. We kissed, our mouths moving together in a feral display of needy hunger. We feasted, desperate to learn each other's taste and feel, memorising every moment.

I walked her back to the bed, helping her move up and on, all without breaking our kiss. Her hungry little moans and whimpers tripped me up, setting me on a self-destructive spiral, bringing the darkness closer to the surface.

"Need you," I growled against her mouth, hands sliding behind her to fumble with the clasp of her bra. "Need to suck these gorgeous breasts."

Honey arched into me, and finally, I unsnapped the flimsy material, pulling it down and tossing it away. Her glorious tits bounced free, my mouth watering at the sight of their fullness.

"Fuck, baby." I immediately dropped my

head, cupping them both and shifting to suck one nipple into my mouth.

Under me, Honey whispered encouragement, her body telling me exactly how much she enjoyed my actions.

Thank fuck.

I pressed long, lingering kisses to each breast, gently sucking and then grazing teeth softly over her sensitised skin. She lost control, bucking and begging, desperate for more.

Don't worry, I'll give you everything.

I moved down her body, worshipping every dip, curve, and hollow I found. Her hands clutched at my hair, and I relished the pinpricks of pain.

I hovered over her abdomen, hooking my fingers into her underwear.

"Gonna eat this pretty pussy now."

"Oh gods," she panted as I stripped her bare.

My mouth descended, covering her hot mound. Her taste exploded on my tongue, and I instantly became lost in the scent, the feel, the taste of her.

"So wet," I praised, shifting to work my thumb against her clit while my tongue moved lower. "Taste so fucking good."

Her body shook under me, more wet coating my mouth, her taste delicious on my tongue. I circled and stroked, finding a rhythm that drew druggy moans and desperate pleas from her lips.

"Please, Tristan. More."

I liked her begging. Found myself wanting more of her needy little whimpers.

"Beg me for it," the words broke free, clawing their way out of my throat. For a moment, I wanted to reel them back in and apologise to the woman I'd fantasised about for years.

But that darker part of me had taken over.

"Please, Sheriff. Please, I need to come. I need you to make me come. Please, Tristan."

Fuck, I liked that. Loved how Honey gripped my hair, pushing me closer. How her mouth parted to give voice to the words I wanted to hear.

"Good girl."

I doubled my effort, my cock now painful against the mattress. I ignored that need, focusing entirely on Honey. Her hips bucked, and a moment later, she came, flooding my mouth, her cries of pleasure filling the room.

I tipped over the edge. Losing all control as I feasted on her, driving her through this orgasm and starting in on the next.

"Need you in me." She tugged my hair, panting. "Hurry, Tristan."

I surged up her body, covering hers with mine.

"Ready?" she asked, her hand snaking between us to grip my cock. I groaned, finding myself unable to speak. I could only stare at her and give a sharp nod.

She drew me to her, positioning me just so. I eased in and nearly came. Hands were a poor substitute for this pleasure.

"Fuck, Baby. So good. Fuck."

Under me, Honey gasped and panted. Muttering words like, "oh gods", and "so big", and "feels amazing."

I tried not to let that go straight to my head, but fuck, I was only human.

I struck up a demanding rhythm, desperate to make this good for her. Around me, her pussy felt like liquid heat. I moved back, hands moving to hold her in place as I shifted up.

"What are you—?"

"I need to see," I grunted. I wanted to see my cock sliding in and out of her pussy. Needed to see me claiming her. I wanted to watch her pussy take me as I ravaged this woman.

She groaned under me, arching back.

We moved together, my cock thrusting into her. Her encouragement egged me on, and soon we were nothing more than violent delights fighting to reach our glorious end together.

"You need more, Baby? You need this big cock filling you up? Marking you?"

"Yes. Oh, please, yes. Harder," Honey panted, her breasts bouncing. "Please, Trist—"

She broke off, her orgasm ripping through her. I felt it, her pussy clamping around me, milking my cock, pulling the orgasm from me.

I came, hard.

Together we rode out our orgasms, my cum coating her insides, her pussy marking my cock.

I could quite happily make love to this woman for the rest of my life. I was wrong before; this had to be what heaven felt like.

I collapsed on top of her, sweaty, panting, and feeling oh-so-good.

Under me, Honey trembled, her gasping breaths loud in the quiet, her body still occasionally clenching around me.

"That was...." she trailed off. "Magnificent."

I chuckled, shifting to kiss her shoulder, and then I remembered. "We didn't use a condom."

"You're clear, I'm clear and I'm on the pill." She lifted one hand to make a dismissive gesture. "We'll get it right next time. Or not."

I rolled, pulling us onto our sides so I could better see her. I brushed the hair away from her face, enjoying the smile that remained on her lips.

"You okay?" I asked, gliding one hand across her side. "I was pretty rough."

Her smile quirked, "I think it's pretty obvious I liked that roughness."

We both chuckled.

"I have pretty dark desires, Honey." I sobered, wanting to be direct and honest. "I can keep them under control most of the time. But you really bring it out of me."

She raised an eyebrow. "Like what?"

Fuck.

"I want to spank you. I want to dominate you. I want to hold you down and fuck you until you can't move. I want to come over your chest and fuck your ass. I want to mark you so no one else will ever touch you."

She shivered, an aroused flush decorating her chest. "I think I can live with all that." Her voice sounded husky.

I blinked. "Really?"

"Oh yeah. But on one condition."

"Anything."

She leaned forward, lips brushing the shell of my ear, hair falling against my cheek.

"Next time, you choke me, just a little."

Fuuuuck.

That dark part of me that had been sated rose back up. My cock immediately hard.

"Suck me," I ordered, fisting her hair. "Gag on my cock first, then we'll see about choking you."

Her body shivered with pleasure, her eyes sparkling. "Yes, Sheriff."

As she slid down my body, making hungry little noises, I praised whatever benevolent beings were listening, thanking them for this bounty of a woman.

6

Honey

True to his word, Tristan had taken me out for breakfast the next morning. Though, to be fair, it had been more like brunch. The guy was obviously making up for lost time. I wasn't going to complain.

We'd gotten together nearly three weeks ago, and I could say quite confidently that this was the happiest I'd been in a long time. Tristan treated me like gold outside the bedroom.

And inside? That was a completely different story.

The man was an insatiable dominant who loved to push me to my limits. And I let him. He has drawn out my deepest, darkest fantasies that I wouldn't trust with anyone else. I liked the contradiction, the good Sheriff in public, the filthy deviant in private. Just thinking about him got my pussy wet.

"Alright, Mrs. Bronze, I think we'll finish there." I helped her off the treadmill and over to our stretch area. "Collins? Can you help Mrs. Bronze cool down?"

Collins looked up from where she crouched beside four-year-old Harry. The toddler lived with spina bifida, and Collins was supporting him to learn how to walk with the help of a tiny walker.

"Of course. Mrs. Bronze, great to see you again."

The elderly lady gave Collins a brisk nod, still panting from her exertions. Mrs. Bronze had experienced a stroke last year. She'd made fantastic progress in regaining mobility but still had a way to go.

"Oh, and say hey to Ella for me," I said. "I look forward to seeing her at yoga on Saturday."

"She's trying to drag her fiancé along."

I snorted, imagining Gunnar, Ella's giant Viking-like fiancé, attending our class. He'd cause a riot among the soccer mums and single ladies.

"Well, wish her luck for me."

Mrs. Bronze had been my last patient for the day, but I still had a mountain of paperwork to get through. I really needed to hire an office administrator to handle this side of the business. With the new extension, we were growing, and I needed to make some decisions about where I wanted to take the clinic.

I worked hard the rest of the afternoon, logging pay slips, following up with outstanding clients, and crunching numbers to work out if I could hire someone to do this for me. If we added another weekend class to the roster, then yeah, I could do that comfortably.

My phone buzzed with an incoming call, and I made the rookie error of answering without checking the caller ID.

"Hello, this is Honey."

"Honey, this is your mother. I'm calling about Thanksgiving."

The blood in my veins ran cold. My spine immediately snapped upright, my shoulders tightening in response.

"I thought you had decided we weren't doing Thanksgiving this year," I said slowly, experience having taught me that nothing I could say would be right in this situation.

She made a dismissive sound. "Plans change. Your brother and sister are coming home. We'll do dinner at the house at six. Ensure you're suitably attired. I've invited the Sheriff."

I blinked. Tristan and I hadn't exactly been keeping our relationship quiet. We'd gone out on dates and seen friends and family around town. Hell, he'd taken me to his mother's a few times, and I'd even had lunch with his brother when Wolf had been in town.

"I didn't realise you knew about me and—"

"Your sister has broken up with the banker. I want her to come back home. Sheriff Rodriguez, while not my first choice, is attractive. And I'm sure with the right guidance, could progress to politics in due course. Also, I've instructed Emily to undergo my juice-only cleanse. Don't offer her any solid food; it would be offensive. See you on Thursday."

She hung up before I could respond. I contemplated calling Tristan, but also knew he was on duty. I settled for a text.

ME

Hey, Mum just called. Said she'd invited you to Thanksgiving?

HOT SHERIFF

Hey, sexy. Yeah, looking forward to doing the meet-the-parents thing.

I bit my lip, wondering if I should clue him in.

ME

I don't think they realise we're a
thing.

HOT SHERIFF

Babe, we're more than a 'thing.'

That warmed me inside and brought a
goofy smile to my face.

HOT SHERIFF

But seriously, if they don't know
by now, then we'll just clue them
in on Thursday.

Uncertainty and anxious fear churned my
stomach. I didn't know how to explain how
crazy my parents could be. I felt the need to
warn him, but I also didn't want him to think
less of me.

ME

My parents are a little intense.
They might not take kindly to us
dating.

I hovered over the screen, waiting for his
reply. I nearly dropped the phone when he
called instead.

"Honey," his voice sounded firm and loving.
"You're overthinking this, Baby."

"I'm really not," I told him earnestly. "They

can be pretty horrible without even trying. Our best option is to decline the invitation and go back to our original plan, dinner at my place."

"I'm not turning down the first invitation to meet your parents. I'm in this for the long haul, Honey. We can't avoid them forever. So, let's make the best of this opportunity. We'll have dinner, announce our relationship, and then eat some turkey."

God, he's sweet. Too bad he's also delusional.

"My sister-in-law is on a juice cleanse. I doubt they'll be serving turkey this year."

There was a beat of silence. "Will there be pie?"

I felt a smile tug at the corners of my mouth at his hopeful tone. "Doubtful. Last year they did a fruit bowl for dessert."

"Those motherfucking monsters!" He sounded so outraged it made me chuckle. "That's a crime against humanity, surely."

My anxiety diminished a little. "I'll have pie waiting for you at home."

"And whipped cream. I have grand plans that involve you and the cream."

My lips quirked as I leaned back in my chair. "Oh, really?"

"Oh, yes." His voice roughened. He made a sound, the phone moving. I waited, knowing our time was short.

"Sorry, babe. I gotta go. You good now?"

"Yeah." The words 'I love you' were on the tip of my tongue, but I swallowed them back down. "I'll see you tonight."

"Your place. I wanna fuck you under that creepy fucking witch in your living room."

The witch was a new purchase and even I had to admit she was fucking creepy. Didn't mean I was going to get rid of her any time soon.

"Later, Honey."

"Bye." I hung up, finding myself in a better mood. All my life I'd been alone while dealing with the low expectations and subpar treatment I received from my parents. Now I had a champion on my side. It felt... nice. Warm. Fuzzy. Like someone actually gave a shit about me.

"Pies," I muttered, navigating to google recipes. "Cream pies."

A knock on the door interrupted my search.

"Come in."

"Hey," Collins poked her head in. "Do you have a minute?"

"For you? Of course."

She came in, bumping the door closed with her hip, her hands wringing slightly as she took a seat.

"You okay?" I asked, leaning forward.

"Yeah, it's just...." She blew out a long breath. "I need some time off."

"Okay. How long?"

"A month. Maybe a little more. I'll take it around our Christmas leave if that works for you?"

I nodded, frowning. "What's going on? Is everything alright?"

Her chin wobbled, tears shimmering on her dark lashes as she ran a hand through her hair.

"You know I want kids, yeah?"

I nodded, my gut clenching at the raw desire in Collins' voice. "I don't think there's ever been any doubt in my mind how great a mother you'll be."

"So here's the thing. I'm married."

I blanched.

"I'm sorry, you're what."

She pressed a hand to her eyes. "I know. I'm... I'm sorry. I didn't tell anyone because... well, it's complicated. We've been estranged for a while. Five years, actually. And it's been hard. Difficult. He's... and I'm...." She shook her head.

Shaking off my own hurt and shock at her revelation, I reached out, squeezing her hand. "What do you need?"

"I need to go to London. We have a prenup, and it's.... It's pretty airtight. I need to see if I can talk my husband into agreeing to father my child."

My eyebrows shot up.

"Not like that," she rushed to assure me. "IVF. I've looked into it and... it's what I want. I know he doesn't want kids. Or me. But he needs an heir and.... This? This is what I want."

"And if he says no?" I asked, my heart breaking for my friend.

"Then it's over. It's been over for years. I know that but... I guess I hoped...." She shook her head. "It doesn't matter now."

I stood, coming to wrap her in a tight hug. "Whatever you need, Collins. You take all the time in the world. You need me to get on a plane and travel with you? I'll do it? You need me to kill this guy? I listen to true crime podcasts, we can work out how to bury a body that will never be discovered."

She let out a watery laugh. "You're the best. You know that, right?"

"I know."

She pulled back, brushing a stray tear from her cheek. "Now, you need to tell me all about the delicious hunk of man meat that keeps dropping by for lunch. Does the wrapping match the reality?"

I sighed my cheeks heating. "This calls for tequila."

"Well, break it out, girlfriend. 'Cause I want to hear *all* the details."

With a laugh, I pulled the bottle out of my bottom drawer. "Please tell me all the clients have left."

"Yeah, and I waved off Harper an hour ago."

I grinned, pulling the cap off and handing the bottle over. "Then bottoms up, Mumma-to-be. This might be your last drink for a few years."

Collins stared at the liquid for a moment, the hope on her face almost too painful to view.

"I'll cheers to that."

7

Tristan

My mum had driven down to the South Island to spend Thanksgiving with Wolf. This was our first Thanksgiving without Dad, and she'd decided to spend it away from home. The memories were still too fresh.

I'd offered to come, but she'd told me they'd be fine. They were going to dinner at some swanky restaurant, then out to catch a movie. My brother had assured me he'd ensure she had a good time.

I glanced for the fifteenth time in a minute at my phone, checking for SOS messages.

"Hey, eyes on the road, pal," Honey told me, her hand reaching out to squeeze my thigh.

"Don't worry so much. They're both grown adults. If they need you, they'll call."

I blew out a breath. "You're right. It's just fucking hard to remember that when you're used to being the one they rely on."

She made a sympathetic sound, reading me clearly. "Are you okay?"

"Yeah, I mean, you're never gonna be completely fine after you lose a parent. There's this aching hole inside me which will always miss my dad." I tapped my chest. "But I gotta move on. Can't be stuck in this loop of grief forever. He wouldn't want that for me. For us."

"I get that. But it's okay to have bad days. I'm here if you need me."

I reached over, finding her hand and lacing our fingers together. "He'd have loved you."

"Your dad?"

"Mmm." I withdrew my hand, using it to hit the turn signal and cruise into her parent's street. "He liked you back in high school. Always said that you were gonna change the world."

"I—I never knew that."

I chuckled, pulling into her parent's drive. I parked, then turned to look at her in the dim light. Her face was done up, make-up smoky, so she said. It made her eyes look wider, her lips cherry red and infinitely kissable.

"That slight crush? I may have talked about you ad nauseam at home." I gave her a crooked grin. "I had no chill as a teenager."

"One could say you have no chill now," she teased, shuffling over in her seat. "But I like it."

"Good." I leaned in, pressing a kiss to her mouth. "Cause you're gonna be stuck with it for a long time."

We separated, and she reached up, rubbing her thumb over my lips to remove her lipstick. When satisfied, we exited the car, walking down the long drive.

I'd never be able to afford a property on this side of town. Rich, decadent, and white. Those were the words that sprung to mind when you looked at the houses around here. I didn't know if it was a rich thing or a coastal thing or maybe a designer thing, but all the damn houses were white and ostentatious.

We reached the porch, and Honey stopped, pressing the bell. That struck me as strange. I'd never knocked on my parent's door. You rapped a knuckle as you swung inside, welcomed by smells of food, hugs, and laughter. But Honey had warned me they were formal people.

The door swung open, revealing a man dressed in prim black and white standing in the doorway.

"Ms. Jameson, Sheriff Rodriguez, do come in."

"Hi Claude," Honey greeted, stepping through the doorway. "Are they in the parlour?"

"Yes, Miss. Can I get you a drink?"

Honey glanced my way in question.

"A beer would be great."

"Just a glass of soda for me, thanks."

He took our coats and then headed off to the kitchen.

"Was that a butler?" I asked in a low voice as we paused in the entry, Honey adjusting her hair.

"Yeah. Claude. He's been with the family for five years now. Good guy puts up with a lot."

I'd had no idea butlers still existed until today.

"How do I look?" Honey turned to me, holding her arms out at her sides and doing a little spin.

The dark burgundy dress hugged every one of her curves. It dipped into a v at the front, revealing just a hint of the tempting globes of her breasts. She wore fishnet stockings on her legs and fuck-me heels on her feet. She'd done something to her hair, causing it to fall in soft ringlets about her face and spill down her back and across her cleavage. She looked like sex in heels.

"Gorgeous," I told her, not even trying to hide the guttural tone in my voice.

She flushed, waving a hand at me. "Shhh, you'll get me all worked up."

I reached over, pulling her to me, brushing one curl back from her face. "Good. It'll make you think of all the naughty things I want to do to you tonight." I bent to gently nip her collarbone.

She leaned into me, but I shifted back, leaving her wanting.

"Come on, sexy. Let's go meet your parents." I linked fingers with her, keeping our hands clasped as she led me through their house.

Palatial was the word I'd use to describe this place. But also cold and soulless. Honey's little townhouse with its plethora of decorations felt like home compared to this giant behemoth. A few delicately placed ornaments sat here and there, but it looked contrived rather than celebratory.

We paused by the parlour door. Honey straightening beside me. I took in the scene, immediately noting the formal attire. Honey's brother sat with his wife on the far sofa, delicate wine glasses in hand. Her father cradled a tumbler of something dark beside the fire, while her mother and sister sat on a loveseat, chatting.

The scene looked like something out of a

TV drama. Everyone dressed up and positioned just so. I'd let Honey choose my outfit and felt immediately glad she'd insisted on the crisp chinos, dark purple button-up, and a sports jacket. I had a feeling I'd need all the advantages I could get.

"Sheriff!" Mrs. Jameson rose gracefully from the loveseat, gliding across the floor toward us, her hands outstretched in welcome. "We're so pleased you could join us."

I was forced to drop Honey's hand to take her mother's. "Thank you for having me, Mrs. Jameson."

"Oh, please. Call me Helen."

She led me to the fireplace, introducing me to Honey's father, Richard. I knew her brother Calvin and her sister Willodean from school. I hadn't met her sister-in-law Emily but immediately disliked her. There was something about her that rubbed me the wrong way.

"Hey, sis," Calvin called, stalking across the room to wrap his sister in a hug. "Great to see you."

Honey's arms went around her brother, and they swayed for a moment. Willodean followed, hugging her sister and whispering something I didn't catch in her ear. Honey laughed, sending her sister a wink.

"Willodean, come meet the Sheriff," Helen

ordered. She sent me a dazzling smile. "My eldest daughter is a financier, you know. We're very proud."

Willodean held out a hand. "Sheriff, I hear through the grapevine you're dating my sister."

I took her hand, giving it a firm shake. "That's right." I sent a grin Honey's way. "So far, so good. If it keeps going the way it is, we might be heading toward something more permanent."

Honey made a dismissive gesture. "Flatterer."

We all chuckled. I turned back to Helen and immediately stiffened. Over her shoulder, Emily looked like she'd swallowed a lemon while Richard stared at his youngest child, a mystified expression on his face.

"Honey? You're dating *Honey*?" Helen asked, her hands now hovering above her pearl necklace.

"That's right, Ma'am." I reached out, pulling Honey to my side and wrapping an arm around her. I didn't like the vibe in the room. It felt cold and uncomfortable.

"But she's.... But—" Helen's hands flapped for a moment, her mouth opening and shutting like a fish.

"Fat," Emily drawled from behind her. "That's the word you're looking for, Helen. Fat."

"Yes, I mean—"

Calvin and Willodean protested while Emily and Helen explained all the reasons we didn't belong together. Richard stood mute, his gaze locked on his glass the entire time.

Beside me, Honey didn't react–which told me everything I needed to know.

"Come on." I turned us toward the entry.

"Where are we going?"

"Home."

She blinked up at me, little confused frown lines marring her forehead. "We're leaving?"

"We're definitely not staying after that. I won't have you talked down to, abused, or offended. We're done."

Honey followed me, letting me put her in my car, then rush back for our things. Helen stood at the door, Claude holding our coats at the ready.

"Tristan, I must say, this is very disappointing. I expected so much better from the Sheriff of our town."

"And I expected better from the parents of the woman I love." I shook my head, pulling our coats into my arms. "Your daughter is talented, beautiful, intelligent, and a magnificent human being. She works hard to improve the lives of other people. Her business is thriving, and her colleagues and friends adore her." I turned, moving toward the door. "If you can't appreciate that, then you don't deserve her."

I left, shutting the door firmly behind me. I gently draped the coat over her in the car and immediately pulled out of the driveway, heading back to town. Silence dominated the small space, my anger raging around us like a small storm.

"Tristan?" Honey finally asked as we hit her street.

"I'm not sorry," I burst out, anger still sizzling in my veins. "But I'm not going to apologise for leaving or offending your parents. I'm done with them. You want me to take another approach, fine. We'll do it. But the ground rules are they're not to speak to you like that. They, or that fucking harpy you call a sister-in-law, speak to you like that again, and I'm walking us out."

"Tristan," Honey said again as we pulled into her driveway.

"I'm serious, Honey. I won't have anyone disparage you. You're worth more than that lot combined. What the fuck were they thinking? Don't they see you're a motherfucking queen? You're the best woman I know. You're caring and gorgeous and clever and witty—"

"Tristan!"

"What?"

She raised a hand, cupping my jaw. Her eyes

were warm but a little wet. Anger crackled again, seeing those unshed tears.

"I'm trying to tell you I love you," she whispered.

For a moment, her words didn't penetrate; the world still bathed in red rage. But then they registered, and all the anger drained from me, leaving behind only heat.

"Baby," I whispered, a hand creeping up to fist in her hair. "You have the worst timing ever."

She snorted. "You just literally pulled me from a situation I have been in a hundred times before. I would have put up with it, the backhanded comments, the overt insults because that's what I do."

"No more," I ordered. "You deserve better."

"I know." She gave me a smile that could only be described as brilliant. "Thank you, Tristan."

"Babe, I didn't do anything."

She hummed her agreement, but I knew she only did it to pacify me. Her lips met mine, and we kissed in the dark car.

"Love you too, Honey," I murmured against her lips.

"I know."

The atmosphere surrounding us quickly changed. "Get inside."

I don't think either of us had ever moved so quickly before.

On the fluffy rug before her gas fire and under the creepy fucking gaze of that damned witch, I laid her down. I peeled clothing from her body, dancing kisses across her skin as I revealed her glorious nakedness. I needed to mark her, to sear her taste into my memory, to etch every beautiful inch of her across my heart.

She squirmed under my mouth, my hands holding her in place.

"Please, Tristan. Please," she begged as I teased her. Her clit pulsed under my tongue, her taste overwhelming all my senses.

"Please, what?" I ordered harshly.

"Please, Sheriff," she corrected. "Please fuck me, Sheriff."

I surged up, pinning her down, taking her in one violent move. She jerked under me, a cry of pure pleasure bursting from between her lips.

"Yes! Thank you, Sheriff. Yes!"

I grunted, that anger from earlier resurging. Not at her, never at Honey. No, at the fact her so-called family could be so cruel to this amazing woman, to the point she'd learned to accept it. I used it, funnelled that anger, and fanned it until I was in a sexual frenzy.

Honey, instead of being intimidated by my intensity, relished it. She bit me, scratched my back, and cried out again and again as I made her come.

"Tristan, I can't—I can't take any more—"

"One more," I demanded, sweat dripping down my brow, my arms straining as I worked my cock against her clit. "Give it to me."

She moaned, arching under me, her legs granting me greater access.

"Whose pussy is this?"

"Yours," she groaned, her hips now jerking under me.

"Who owns you, Honey?"

"You do."

"Who loves you?"

"You do."

"Who do you love?"

"You. I love you, Tris—" she broke off as her pussy violently clenched around my cock. Honey's body shattered, shaking un-controllably as the orgasm tore through her. I came, thrusting into her with heaving groans before collapsing beside her on the rug.

We panted beside each other, my fingers finding and entwining with hers.

"If I didn't love you before—"

We both chuckled. Silence fell between us, easy and comfortable. My stomach grumbled in the quiet.

Honey lifted onto one elbow, chuckling. "We haven't eaten."

"We can order something."

"Chinese?"

"Sounds great."

We dressed in PJs and watched cheesy Netflix holiday movies while eating Kung Pao Chicken and wontons.

"You know," Honey said later, her head cradled against my chest as we lay sprawled across the couch. "I made pies."

"Pie?" I asked, perking up.

"Pies plural."

"What kind of pies?"

"Chocolate cream, pumpkin, brown butter apple, and cherry. I also have plain ice cream and whipped cream and berries if you'd prefer. I wasn't sure what you liked."

"You made me four pies?" I sat up quickly, dislodging Honey and causing her to roll off the couch and onto the floor.

"Oof," she grunted, blinking up at me before bursting into laughter. "Tristan!"

"Sorry." I reached down, helping her up. "It's just—you made me four pies?"

"I wasn't sure what you wanted. Caleb said you always turn down all the baked goods at the precinct, so I didn't know what flavours to make."

I shook my head, "Babe, that's because those are from other women looking to hook their claws into me."

She tilted her head to one side, a teasing smile lighting her face. "So, you do like my baked goods?"

"Oh, yeah."

"Including my muffin top?" she asked, pointing at her belly.

"Especially your muffin top." I bent down, pressing kisses to her belly. "But my favourite is always gonna be you in a cupcake outfit." She giggled as I nuzzled her neck. "And I know I'm gonna love every piece of those pies."

"How do you know?" she asked, slightly breathless.

"Because I love sweet things. And if they taste anything like you, then I'll be in heaven."

She groaned, swatting me away. "That was terrible."

"Come, give me some sugar," I ordered.

She obliged, leaning in for a kiss.

"Love you, Honey."

"Love you too, Sheriff."

8

Honey

I'd gone overboard for Christmas.

I knew this. The clinic was filled with tasteful decorations, including a new candy cane and sugar cookie scent that I couldn't help but love. At home, my house looked like Santa's workshop. Little elves hid here and there, tinkering with toys in various stages of construction. I'd invited my neighbours over for my annual pre-Christmas dinner —their kids had loved it.

But this?

I tilted my head, biting my lip as I inspected my work.

Tristan is gonna freak.

It was Christmas Eve, and I'd promised to spend it at his house. I always closed the clinic at noon on Christmas Eve, so we'd planned to have lunch together. Instead, Tristan had called to say he'd been held up with an incident. The hours in between had been dangerous. So very, very dangerous.

I'd spent the afternoon browsing stores for last-minute Christmas gifts and left with a car full of gifts and decorations. I'd then spent half the afternoon and most of the early evening baking and decorating his house.

Prior to this afternoon, Tristan had put up a tree–a fake plastic monstrosity that I'd immediately needed to decorate in a rainbow theme. He'd also pulled an ancient wreath from somewhere, hanging it proudly on his door.

But now? Now his home looked like something out of a Christmas movie. Presents were placed strategically about the house; two nutcrackers five feet high book ended his staircase. I'd hung embroidered stockings with care above his fireplace—one for each of his family members—and laid a train track under his Christmas tree. I'd swapped out all his dishcloths and towels with Christmas colours and themes. I'd hung mistletoe, draped leaf and berry garlands, and even placed little removable Santa hat stickers on some of his wall photos.

He is so gonna freak.

Decision made, I reached for some bunting, determined to remove all evidence of my craziness before Tristan returned.

Then the damned front door opened.

"Babe, I'm home."

"Damn," I muttered, struck by indecision. Did I try to distract him with boobs? Did I start ripping down decorations and hide them under cushions before he entered the room? Or did I yell surprise and not give him the opportunity to be disappointed?

The decision was made for me when he entered the living room. He stopped, his eyes widening as he took in the scene.

"Is that a poinsettia?"

"Yes!" I squeaked, immediately snapping my mouth shut and wringing my hands. The beautiful plant on his hearth added a bright splash of red to the room.

Tristan stepped in further, looking around, his hands settling on his hips. His beautiful hair flopped over his forehead. His normally tan skin had a lighter shade to it now that we were in the depth of winter.

I watched him take in the train set, size up the nutcracker soldiers, and stop when he saw the stockings hanging above the fireplace.

"Honey...." He walked over, fingering the one that read 'Dad.'

I followed, wrapping my arms around him. "I know he's gone, but he's still a big part of your family. I thought maybe we could start a tradition where you all put a little something in there that reminds you of him, and we can pull them out at dinner to remember."

He dropped the stocking, letting it fall back into place. Tristan turned to me, his dark eyes warm. "I love it. I love the idea, I love the decorations, I love you."

He kissed me, one hand cupping my jaw, the other wrapped around my back, holding me close. This kiss tasted of warm chocolate, bittersweet memories, and comfortable nights in each other's arms.

We broke apart, Tristan pressing his forehead to mine. "I was gonna surprise you with an early gift, but I'm not sure it'll top this."

I brightened; my interest immediately peaked. "An early gift?"

"Mmhmm, it's in the hall."

I let him go, practically sprinting to the front entry. In the entry, I found my brother and sister, both grinning. Calvin held a giant box, while Willodean held pizzas.

"You guys," I pressed my hands to my mouth, vibrating with happiness. "You came!"

"Of course," my brother told me, stamping the snow off his boots. "We weren't gonna miss this."

"Miss—?" A tiny squeak from Calvin's box interrupted me.

He set it down at my feet, beaming. "Open it up, sis."

I dropped to my knees, gently peeling back the cardboard folds. Inside, nestled in a bunch of towels, sat the smallest, skinniest, saddest sleeping puppy I'd ever seen.

"Oh!" I whispered, reaching out a fingertip to trace her little spine. "You're so small."

"Rescue," Tristan told me. "That thing I got caught up with? Puppy farm. Illegal breeders who got busted. All the dogs and pups were farmed out to various rescue groups, which is why it took so long."

Tristan dropped to his knees beside me, lifting the small pup from the box. "All except this little girl. Her mumma rejected her, which is why she's so tiny. But she's a fighter. Needs a good feed, but the vet cleared her to come home." Tristan handed her to me. "Figured, if she needs a mumma, you'd be the best one available."

I cradled the small pup in my arms, gently stroking her soft little fur.

"She's so tiny and light," I whispered, scarcely able to bear the sight of her. My heart was exploding all over the place, my ovaries practically bursting with maternal instincts.

Willodean returned, having dropped the pizzas off in the kitchen. "She needs a name."

I watched as the puppy's teeny eyes opened, blinking up at me sleepily. She sighed, then settled back in my arms with a little yawn. "How about... Cupcake?"

Tristan chuckled, pressing a kiss to the side of my head. "It's perfect."

"Oh!" I looked over at Tristan, stricken. "But I don't have stockings for everyone!"

He grinned, then reached into his coat pocket, pulling out three stockings. Two with Calvin and Willodean's names embroidered on the outside and a smaller one with a little paw print on it.

"How did you...?"

"Babe, because I know you." He cupped my cheek, kissing my forehead. "Now go hang these." He passed me the stockings. "I'll bring in the puppy bed."

That night my brother announced he was divorcing Emily, my sister announced she was dating a woman named Lou, and Tristan asked me to move in with him. Cupcake slept through the whole thing.

And I had never been happier than I was at that moment.

When life gives you muffin tops, embrace them. Because if I've learned anything, it's that you're delicious just as you are.

EPILOGUE

Tristan

Muffins.

Muffins had taken over my house. They decorated the entry table, the buffet, and the living room couch—cordoned off by a weird pillow and blanket fence that didn't look like it would do shit to stop the dogs from getting to them.

I blinked, rubbing a hand across my eyes sure I had to be imagining this.

Nope, the muffins were still there.

"Honey?" I called, dodging Cupcake and our second dog, Roast Beef. I pushed a row of chew toys out of the way and neatly stepped around a teddy bear picnic in progress. "Honey?"

"In the kitchen!"

I followed the smell of muffins and the sound of laughter, finding my mother, brother, and wife in the kitchen. Muffins and cupcakes took up every free surface.

"What—?"

"Babe!" Honey skipped to my side, kissed my cheek then danced back to stand in the middle of our kitchen. "Look!" She swung her arms out, making jazz hands at the baked goods.

"I'm looking. I just don't know what I'm looking at."

"It was your mum's idea."

Mum ducked her head, making a dismissive flick of her hand. "Oh, it's nothing. I just thought we could do a bake sale for your open day. Maybe raise some money for a new couch for your break room."

I ran a hand through my hair, taking in the mountains of food that decorated our kitchen. "I think we'll make enough to renovate the damned break room."

They all laughed.

"Here." Honey handed me a half-decorated cupcake. "Eat up, Sheriff."

"Daddy?"

I turned, seeing our little Nicole standing in the doorway. She rubbed her eyes, looking sleepy.

"Hey, sweetheart." I bent, pulling her into my arms. "You just wake up?"

She nodded, snuggling close, her little arms wrapping around my neck.

"We had a great tea party earlier that ran through normal nap time," Wolf told me around a mouth full of muffin. "General Nicole here was deciding on the taxes to allot the Teddy Bear Kingdom. She made some good decisions, and we just couldn't stop in the middle of the council meeting. Wouldn't be good for the Kingdom."

I rolled my eyes, holding my little girl closer. "She's three."

"Never too early to develop a love of STEM. Or know your leadership appeal."

"Again, she's three."

"Nicole, how old are you?" Wolf asked.

She held out a hand, holding up three fingers.

"And if we add one more, how old will you be next year?"

She held up another finger for four.

Wolf beamed. "See? The girl is a genius."

"And her Uncle is biased," Honey sang, piping icing onto bare cupcakes. "Babe, do you want to get her fed?"

"Can do."

I fed and washed our little munchkin, letting her play for a while before getting her settled for bed. I finished with a story, tucking my baby in. Roast Beef, named for the meal we had on the night we'd found out we were pregnant, and Cupcake settled on their beds outside Nicole's room. Her overly enthusiastic guardians.

I returned to find my kitchen somewhat back to rights. The baked goods still occupied most surfaces, but the dishes were clean, and the goodies were all packed in boxes or Tupperware that I had no idea we even owned. I found my beautiful wife in the living room, decorating cookies.

"Hey, you wanna order something? The kitchen's now officially muffin-owned territory, and your family bailed." She piped two circles on either end of the cookie, adding links from one to the other, turning it from a blue blob to a blue background with handcuffs.

"That's cool," I looked over her other decorations. "I married a talented woman."

She glanced up, beaming at me. "And I married one hot Sheriff."

I chuckled, settling down beside her. "I love you, Honey."

"Love you too, Babe."

I looked around, taking in the numerous

boxes she'd painstakingly assembled, all to get my guys and me a new couch.

"Nicole's asleep." I ran a hand down her leg. "How about I put that order in, and you take a break to relax?"

She raised an eyebrow at me, pausing in her decorating. "What did you have in mind?"

"You've been working so hard, how about a massage?"

Her eyes lit, her cheeks immediately flushing. "Yes, please."

I pulled her up, leading her to the stairs. "Go get ready."

She started to turn, but I stopped her with a gentle tug on her wrist. She tilted her head in question.

"What do you say?"

She bit her lip, her eyes dark with desire. "Yes, *Sheriff*."

"Good girl." I smacked her on the butt as she passed, causing her to squeal and laugh as she jogged up the stairs. "Hurry, Honey. I got a mighty need to see you flushed and relaxed."

"Promises, promises!"

And that's how we ended up with a brother for Nicole, a new couch for the precinct, and our next dog named Muffin.

***

If you loved this book, be sure to check out the bonus slice of life on my website!

Up next is The Mrs. Clause, featuring Collins as she reconnects with her husband... will they have a happily ever after?

*You can continue the entire series by checking them out on my website at
www.EvieMitchell.com
If you enter the code **EBOOK10** you can get 10% off your purchase from my website.*

ABOUT THE AUTHOR

Evie Mitchell is a thirty-something romance author (she/her/hers) living with disability. She believes in inclusion, accessibility, and fierce romance. Her loves include steamy romance novels, her husband, their THREE sausage dogs (heaven help her), and her ever-growing collection of book-related mugs.

As a woman with a diverse work history including in areas such as emergency response, event management, human rights, disability access, and security - her books are filled with true stories (bridezillas), worst-case scenarios (malfunctioning dresses), and her favorite tropes (one-bed).

Evie specialises in fiercely inclusive happily ever afters.

ALSO BY EVIE MITCHELL

Capricorn Cove Series

The Shake-Up

Double the D

Muffin Top

The Mrs. Clause

New Year Knew You

Double Breasted

As You Wish

You Sleigh Me

Resolution Revolution

Meat Load

Larsson Siblings Series

Thunder Thighs

Clean Sweep

The X-list

Reality Check

The Christmas Contract

Dogg Pack Books

Puppy Love

<u>Bad English</u>

<u>The Frock Up</u>

<u>Pier Pressure</u>

All Access Series

Knot My Type

Love Flushed

Nameless Souls MC Series

<u>Runner</u>

<u>Wrath</u>

<u>Ghost</u>

<u>Shield</u>

Elliot Security Series

<u>Rough Edge</u>

<u>Bleeding Edge</u>